ROTTEN SEED - A MURDER TALE

IT IS JUST A BEGINNING.

MANAS KUMAR RAI

This short story book is dedicated to my Mom and Dad, my college friends, and my love for thrilling stories and movies.

Contents

Foreword

Welcome to the thrilling world of a murder mystery! Prepare to enter a world full of danger, thrills, and of course, mystery. As you delve into this story you will be challenged to use your detective skills to uncover the truth behind the crime.

I know you all are clever enough to spot the clues and help me to solve the case. You can see beyond the surface and work out the real motives of the perpetrator. Will you be able to guess the identity of the villain before it is revealed in the last pages of the story??

There will be many twists and surprises as the plot thickens, and your task is to find out who did it and why. Welcome to the exciting world of murder mysteries! Don't trust anyone!!

Preface

I'm not one to believe in curses or fatalism, but the truth is, I never expected to find myself writing a murder novel. The quiet and unremarkable place in Arunachal Pradesh, the place I had often called home, suddenly found itself thrust onto a national stage. A brutal and mysterious murder uncovered a dark secret. I set out, driven by an odd combination of morbid curiosity and to find the answers.

The story that unfolded was deeply disturbing and at times overwhelming. Nothing I had ever seen or read could have prepared me for what I discovered: a decades-old mystery, hidden secrets, powerful adversaries, and a community that had been pulled apart by fear and hatred. I know things just like I was there, so by I used this book as a medium to tell the world about this story.

The journey was not easy, but in time the truth gets uncovered, it is Indian based story with all Indian characters.

Acknowledgements

I would like to take a moment to thank my family and friends for their constant support, encouragement and understanding throughout the writing of this novel. I could not have finished it without their unconditional love and dedication.A special thanks to my editor for her keen eye for detail and for providing the necessary guidance. They spent countless hours reading, discussing and adjusting the story until it was ready for publication.I also want to thank all those who have inspired me along the way. Finally, I would like to express my gratitude to all of you, the readers, for embarking on this journey with me. I hope it has been as enjoyable for you as it has been for me.

~By Author

<h1 style="text-align:center">Prologue</h1>

It was supposed to be a simple day, like all the others. In the small village of Himachal Pradesh, nothing ever really happens. People come and go, going about their lives as best they can. But that day, something changed. Murder was the first sign something was amiss. No one knew the victim, and no one knew who the suspect could be. The police were baffled, and the people of Kino Village were scared. Undoubtedly not one of their own could have been responsible. But as the investigation unfolded, it became clear that someone in Kino villagemust be responsible. Someone had murdered, and someone was hiding the truth. The mystery had to be solved, but who could uncover the truth? Who could put the pieces together and find the killer? Only time would tell if the mystery would be solved, or if the killer would remain forever a mystery.

1

It Begins....

———❤———

"Kehte hai sach dabe paudhe ki tarah hota hai chahe jitna bhi zameen me daba do ,ek din wo bahar aa hi jata hai, par kya ye zaruri hai!"

"It is said that truth is like a buried plant, no matter how much you bury it in the ground, one day it comes out, but is it necessary!"

Hello, my readers in the journey of reading this book I'm going to be your storyteller, as I am not a part of this story. You can understand in this way that I was the watcher of this whole incident. I was present everywhere at every happy and sad moment. Hence, you will all visualize this story according to my point of view. Here we begin... There was a boy Rohit, who used to live in the Kino village, Himachal Pradesh and it was around October's end. Rohit was a boy of height 5'9", with light Indian shade. He was in 11th at the local Government School of Kino Village. He was brilliant since childhood. His father is an electrical engineer and his mom used to work at home and take care of her family. Kino is a small village around 30 km from the main city, so everyone knows each other. Rohit, Rajiv, and Radhika were childhood friends. As we know Rohit was a brilliant student but he was weak in biology. So, he used to wake up every morning at 4.30 AM for his Biology tuition. And he was half asleep while walking on a lonely road that lead to his tuition point. Every single morning he has to walk around 1km on the hilly tracks. Mr. Jay Aggarwal his biology tuition teacher, use to teach in the living room of his house and he works as a Government doctor. And the whole village knows that his wife died a long time ago due to some disease. Every morning it's Rohit's duty to call Rajiv for biology tuition. Rajiv is lazy ass it always took at least 15 minutes to get him ready for tuition. And this is the only reason for getting late in tuition every day. On that day, they both reached tuition late as usual but sir was a little upset. Every day sir used to scold them for getting late in tuition and sir used to tell them about discipline and moral values. But he was quiet on that day and then sir said: "Today don't wanna take the class". We asked what happened. He said: "Nothing". And we got happy and started to pack our bags, then sir said: "No need to leave, today I'm going to tell a story to you all". We were 9 students in a batch, and we all said: "Sir, you seemed tensed no need for a story." Sir said: "I'm not asking you. Just sit down". Then we all get back to our places. But I don't know why there was a foul smell in that room, we all ignored that smell and start to listen to that story.

Mr. Jai Aggarwal

2

The main...

In the morning, a boy named Arjun woke up in a mortuary cabinet; his body was entirely senseless due to the cold temperature. He managed to get out of the cabinet. He was covered in frozen blood, had a broken left arm, the muscle on the back side of the right thigh was snatched, cuts on the back from sharp objects, a broken finger on the right hand, and messy hair. And he was trying to remember what had happened to him. But he was unable to get anything. When he looked in the mirror, he couldn't believe his appearance, so he started crawling on the floor and somehow reached the main door, knocking and banging on it for help.

After 3 hours of continuous effort for help, he fainted, and then, after some time, the lab assistant came in the morning and opened the door. He was in shock and feared that a dead body would come out of the cabinet by itself. But somehow he gathered courage and went close to him. And then he learned that he was alive, so he went outside and called some ward boys to carry him to the hospital. And then the doctor admits him to the ICU. After 4 hours of continuous operation, the doctor said, "He is out of danger." and he is at rest now. So don't disturb him." All his vitals were too low. And the doctor also said that: "Someone has beaten him brutally and intentionally, and I have never seen such a case in my career." After 3 days of unconsciousness, he suddenly woke up and started shouting, but his vocals were partially damaged, as said by the doctor; someone had pierced 12 stitching needles in his vocal cord. That's why he was unable to speak properly. And in the hospital, due to past trauma, he started screaming, which hurt his vocal cords. He started scratching the hand of the doctor, crying, and wanting to talk about something.

As I can see, he was not crying about his physical pain. And after seeing this kind of behavior, the doctor gave him a little dosage of a sleep injection. And then Hritik called Arjun's mother, but she was not receiving the phone calls. So Hritik called Samaira and told her the whole story; then Samaria came to the hospital, but she was not able to see Arjun's condition. And they both decided to go to Arjun's house. They saw that it was locked. They both were tense and then decided to file a missing person complaint. At night, they both reach the nearest police station and file a missing person complaint about Arjun's mother.

3

The FIR...

Arjun was 5 years old when his father passed away. He works for a plastic manufacturing company, and in a blast, he passed away. Arjun can't explain how much he loves his mother because he only has one parent.His mother was everything.

When Hritik and Samaira reached the police station, they were so tensed about Arjun's mother. Then they both asked the constable for help; they were gasping. Then the constable took them to the SI cabin. They were so frightened and tensed that they started telling everything to the SI at the same time. But when SI was unable to understand, he said, "Please!" "One at a time." Then Samaira told everything about his friend's condition and about his missing mom. SI told the constable to register their FIR. And the constable asked about his mother's details like height, face shade, hair color, or any unique idenification, and Hritik said yes, she had a mole on the left palm. And she is about 5'7".

The police then immediately began working on this case. First, they went to Arjun's house, which, as we know, was locked. Then, the police asked their neighbour about

Arjun and his mother. But all the neighbours denied it. Police did not give up hope, despite the fact that they had been unable to find the clue until now.

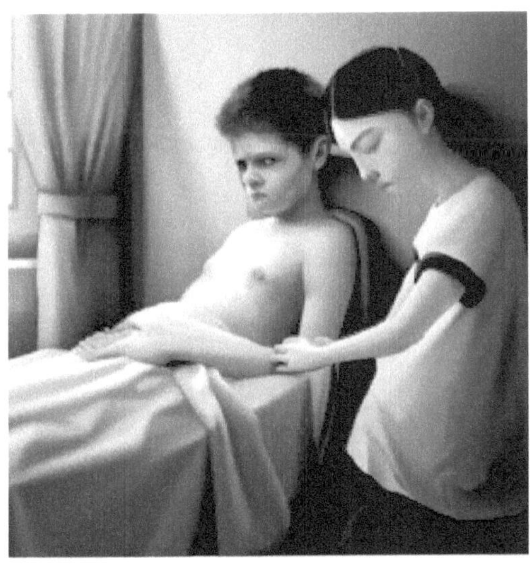

Arjun and Samaira in City Hospital

Then Hritik gets a phone call from the hospital saying that Arjun's condition is much better now and he is recovering very fast. Hritik was full of joy; he asked Samaira to come with him to the hospital. and they both went to the hospital. He can see everything, but he is mute. His left broken arm is now in much better condition, but one finger of the right hand is damaged forever. He was avoiding Hrithik because he did not like him. After knowing all this, Hritik was always there in his support. He couldn't eat properly because of his right-hand finger. Whenever Hritik comes in front of Arjun, he wants to say something to him. The police then entered the hospital and went to Arjun's cabin to check on him and inform him that they were searching for a dead body.

4

Doom of one's Life...

———◦♡◦———

Then on the next day, Rohit came to tuition, and Aggarwal sir continued the story when the police came into the hospital and took him to the emergency room. The police then came and sat down near Arjun's table and asked him about his health, and then they said that they had found a body; Arjun's eye was filled with tears. He started crying, and the police asked him or any one of them to come and check the body, so Samira and Ritik went with the police. When they reached the mortuary room, they both couldn't resist the smell of formalin in that room. The police then asked the lab assistant to lead them to the body, which was in terrible condition, with the muscles of the right thigh scratched and it appearing that it had been eaten. And the hair of the front part was snatched; someone pulled her hair so roughly that her backside and her neck from the back were scratched by some sharp objects, and many marks of defence were there. It seems like she tried very hard to get rid of that place. Samaira couldn't resist that view, so she went outside the walk-in room and vomited. Hritik was not in a state to accept that his aunt was no more. Then he tries to find the mole in her left palm, but both hands are covered in frozen blood, so he calls the cops to see if there is a mole in her left hand. And the following day, they got the information, and the doctor had found a mole in the left palm. Arjun was in shock; he left, taking meals, medicines, and everything. And for some urgent reason, Hritik has to go back to his home, but Samira was always there with the urgent at the hospital; she used to convince him every day and night to take his regular meals and medicines. Sometimes all night Urdu used to cry, but Samaira never got frustrated; she was always there for him. She holds his hand and helps him to walk, and after months of practice, Arjun was finally able to walk, but the finger of his right hand was broken forever. And then Arjun gets discharged from the hospital when Samaira takes him home. But everything in his home reminds Arjun of his mother. Then Samaira helped him settle down, and Samaira left for her home.

And after weeks, when Samaira came back to meet Arjun, she couldn't believe her own eyes: Arjun was so weak, he again started to leave his meals and medicines, and he was depressed as well. Then Samaira didn't wait for a second; she packed all Arjun's bags and took him to her house. And then Aggarwal sir said tomorrow is Sunday, so we will continue the end part on Monday.

5

The Twist...

———♡———

On Sunday, Rajiv came to Rohit's house to have fun. They went on a bike ride, and then Radhika joined them in between. They went from the adventure town to the main city. They played water polo games, shooting games, and volleyball, ate lots of food, and had fun. Then a twist came into Rohit's life. He got mesmerised by the beauty of a girl at the adventure park without thinking about anything. Rohit went towards that girl and said, "Hi, I'm Rohit Sanwal. You?" She just made a weird face expression and left that place, but Rohit was in love at first sight; he was completely lost at that moment. And he was only moving around her that day. She noticed him several times in the park, but in the end she couldn't resist; she came to him and slapped him. Rohit was so lost in her that he didn't feel the pain. She and a group left Park because of Rohit's weird behavior. And then Rajiv and Radhika started to tease him, making fun of him, and while he was coming back towards the village, something was going on. But all three were in a joyful mood and making fun of Rohit for that adventure park girl. They dropped Radhika safely at her home, and then Radhika's mom asked both of them to come home; it was around 8 p.m. at night. They then went to Radhika's house for dinner before leaving around 9 p.m. And they both got home safely. All night, Rohit was thinking about that girl. And after that, he slept, and at night his body was in pain and had a fever because of the water play in the adventure park, so he rested. And his mom was holding him back from playing with water in the months of November and December. And that night was so terrifying. Because of the heavy rain and wind, all of the windows were simply thumping. And six candles were there in Rohit's room; it was a silent place at night, and his mom was taking care of him. He also drank a hot vegetable soup. Then he slept again. And until morning, he was feeling much better and eager to reach tuition because he wanted to hear the whole story. And, in order to end the suspense in the morning, he packed his tuition bags, and Rohit witnessed a miracle. That day, Rajiv (the lazy ass) was already waiting for Rohit outside his home. Rohit was so shocked that he asked. Rajiv Are you okay? Rajiv said, "Yes, of course." I can't handle the suspense anymore. I want to hear that story. "Let's run for tuition." They arrived on time for class and took their seats. Rohit yelled and addressed Aggarwal as sir. After 15 minutes, Rajiv and Rohit decided to go inside the house and call him; they went through all of the rooms. Rajiv shouted, "Oh, hell!" Rohit came, and they saw that his teacher was dead. The walls of the bedroom were covered in blood. There was a gun in the right hand of Mr. Aggarwal, sir; it seems like he shot himself. Rajiv wasn't shocked. He called an ambulance and informed the police. How did a happy, funny, and kind person end up shooting himself and no one knows anything about his mysterious death.

There are many unanswered questions; everything was out of the box, and no one understood anything about his mysterious death.

6

Past Never Leaves You...

After the death of Mr. Aggarwal, Rohit went through severe trauma. His father and mother decided to take him to the nearest city for proper health care and education. So Rohit's family shifted permanently to the nearest city. Rohit had already taken weeks to recover from the death scenes. Sometimes he used to scream at night or start crying, but approximately after one month, he was able to get back to his normal lifestyle. He enrolled in an English-medium school and, against all odds, began his studies in the 11th grade. And Rajiv and Radhika were always missing him. All was going well. Then, when Rohit made the decision to meet Rajiv and Radhika the next weekend, The following Sunday morning, Rohit went to the keynote village and met Rajiv and Radhika. They both were surprised to see him, so they again planned to go to the adventure park just like the old days as they were planning for this. Rohit's trauma hit back. Mr. Gabald comes to mind when he sees those scenes in the village. He started to precipitate, and his hands were shivering. He fell down on the floor. Rajiv called the ambulance to take him to the government hospital. Then the senior doctor at that government hospital referred him to the city hospital. Then doctor me. He was examined and given an injection to put him to sleep. Then Rohit came back to his normal state. after about three hours. His mom and dad came to the hospital. Rajiv and Radhika were already there in the city hospital. Both of them told me what happened. Rohit was released from the hospital after two days. His parents made it clear that he would never return to Keynote Village in his life. Dr. Smith gave him some medications. Also, call him one week after his fourth general checkup. After one week, Rohit's father called in to the city hospital for a general checkup. The receptionist at the hospital said Dr. Kulkarni is on leave. Rohit's father somehow arranged Dr. Kulkarni's personal number and called him. Then Dr. Kulkarni called Rohit to his home. So Rohit's father contacted Dr. Kulkarni's home address, and they rang the doorbell. And then a girl comes up to the door, and the interesting point is that this is the same girl they met at the adventure park. She is the daughter of a doctor. Dr. Kulkarni, the doctor, checked all the reports and said yeah. It's all fine. He is recovering very quickly, and as usual, Rohit lost again after seeing Dr. Kulkarni, who is said to have met my daughter, Shamita Kulkarni. From that day forward, Rohit was smitten with the name and was forever lost in her.Then they started meeting on a daily basis, and a new chemistry and a new love story started in between all these kinds of traumatic periods. They both began to like each other as time passed. Rohit started to talk about his past life. He said that he used to live in Kino Village. Shamita said that she had heard of that place quite a few times, and he said that he was weak in biology, so he used to take tuition from someone named Mr. Aggarwal. Shamita agreed that Jai Sir's bio is excellent. Rohit was shocked, knowing how well she knows him. Out of curiosity, Rohit inquired as to how she knew him, to which she replied, "Months ago, he was her neighbor." Then he left and went to this place, which you call the village. Then Rohit started telling him the whole story of what Aggarwal told him in class. after hearing of the death of Aggarwal. Sir, she wept, saying that the story that occurs and is told to you is not a story anymore.

7

Everything is Connected...

after hearing those things. Rohit became disoriented; he was unable to understand anything. He became disoriented and collapsed on the ground. When I looked at him, he had tears in his eyes and was drowning in the sound of a nearby flowing body of water. Then Shamita lay down beside him. Rohit asked, "What is your story?" "How do you know Arjun?" Then Shamita replied, "Yeah, he was my dearest and only best friend." Rohit said, "How do you know him?" Shamita replied, "So Mr. Aggarwal, sir, told you about it." Arjun's friend Samaira Rohit casually said, "Yes!" "So what?" "What the hell?" he screamed after a second. And he was not able to believe that situation, so Shamita continued. I, Arjun, and Raj were three friends. Rohit asked, "Raj?" and Shamita told Hritik of your story. Raj Guleria is his full name. We used to go to Aggarwal's uncle's house with my childhood friends; he was such a laid-back guy, and Mrs. Aggarwal's aloo paratha was the best in the world. Raj was mischievous as always; he used to pull my hair and hide my things. He was not bad to her, but he couldn't live without his mischievousness. One day. Arjun gets a fever. Mrs. Aggarwal was so tense because she loves Arjun like a son. We used to have a lot of fun playing on our colony grounds. What happened to this cute and sweet family? Rohit said that all that is happening today is that no one is here. "No, no," said Shamita. Arjun died a couple of weeks ago. Rohit was shocked. He said the family was told that he was recovering very fast, and some of that said yes, he died for no reason and no one knows that. Shamita had a good enough flow of story to warrant looking back; Rohit felt like someone was staring at him, so he stood up and looked around, but he didn't see anything. He was in a hurry; he'd grab Shamita's hand and ask her to leave; he couldn't understand anything, and they both left, then he dropped. She went home, and Rohit went to his home. Rohit's mom and dad went to Shimla for some office work. The next day, around 10 a.m., Dr. Guleria called Rohit and said, "Who is this?" This is the last dialled number in Shamita's phone. "Yes," Rohit replied, "but what happened and who are you?" I'm Dr. Guleria, a doctor, and Shamita had a serious car accident. She was on her way, and a truck was behind the car. Rohit was just silent and shoving. Then Dr. Guleria told him to come home right now. Rohit stated that my parents were out of town, and Guleria stated that there were no problems. I'm providing you with transportation facilities after half an hour from when I write. and took Rohit to the hospital after reaching the hospital. Rohit went to the mortuary room. Dr. Guleria was there, and Shamita's body was lying on that stretcher. Rohit couldn't see that he wept. He cried so hard that Dr. Guleria came near him to sympathise with him, but no one could see, so Dr. Guleria closed the door, and as soon as Dr. Guleria closed the door, Shamita woke up. And Rohit said: "What the hell?" Shamita asked what makes you so stupid. Rohit couldn't understand anything; he was shocked and angry simultaneously, and Rohit shouted at Shamita. on and tried to leave, but he couldn't. Dr. Guleria locked the door and threw the keys somewhere in the room. Rohit got frightened and said, "Why, Shamita, why?" Are you doing this to me? "We love each other, right?" Shamita smiled and said, "No, baby." You only love me. "I only love blood." And he stabbed Rohit in the right thigh with a knife. And blood started flowing out, and Samita was licking her blood from Rohit's thigh. It's a revolting scene for me to see Rohit screaming in agony. Dr. Guleria stood at the main door of the room, keeping an eye on what was going on outside. "Why did you do this?" Rohit asked. Arjun was your true friend. Samitha said, "He was more than a friend to me." I proposed to him, but he rejected me for someone else. So I couldn't. So I called him at Dr. Guleria's uncle's house. And she laughed loudly and said, "I killed him, and Guleria's uncle took him to the mortuary cabinet." But I'm not sure how that cretin survived. At the hospital, he always used to see Raj and try to tell him about me and Dr. Guleria. Rohit said, "What was the fault of Mrs. Aggarwal?" Rohit asked how Mr. Aggarwal died, since he was not in the city at the time. Dr. Guleria said, "Mrs. Aggarwal just came with something urgent to my home on that day, so she had to die." Then they both smiled and jumped on Rohit's body, scratching him and eating all the muscles from all sides. And just like vampires, they ate him, and Rohit died. And they disposed of that body. It was such an unknown and weird death. Now the question is: Who killed Dr. Aggrawal? Or was it a suicide? And how did Rohit die? Why does Ritik need to go home right away? Dr. Guleria aided Shamita for what reason? Is Raj unaware of his father's actions?

Now the question is: Who killed Dr. Aggrawal? Or was it a suicide? And how did Rohit die? Why does Ritik need to go home right away? Dr. Guleria aided Shamita for what reason? Is Raj unaware of his father's actions?